W9-CNC-354

Friendship
Across Arctic Waters

Top: Matt Metcalf, Ben Rowe, Ernie James, Russell Rowe, Derek Martin, and Stephen Busch. Bottom: David Larson, Jake Holee, Seth Metsger, Arlo Davis, and Sean McMillan.

Friendship
Across Arctic Waters

Alaskan Cub Scouts
Visit Their
Soviet Neighbors

by Claire Rudolf Murphy   photographs by Charles Mason

Lodestar Books   Dutton   New York

to the people of Provideniya,

especially Svetlana Linnikova and the Young Pioneers;

Cubmaster Glenn Martin and the Nome Cub Scouts;

and our supportive spouses,

Julie and Murph

Library of Congress Cataloging-in-Publication Data

Murphy, Claire Rudolf.
Friendship across Arctic waters: Alaskan Cub Scouts visit their Soviet neighbors / by Claire Rudolf Murphy; photographs by Charles Mason. — 1st ed.
p.   cm.
"Lodestar books."
Summary: Describes the Fourth of July trip of eleven Cub Scouts from Alaska to Provideniya, a small town in the Soviet Far East.
ISBN 0-525-67348-2
1. Cub Scouts—Alaska—Nome—Juvenile literature. 2. Cub Scouts—Journeys—Soviet Union—Juvenile literature. 3. Soviet Far East (R.S.F.S.R.)—Description and travel—Juvenile literature. 4. Soviet Union—Description and travel—Juvenile literature. [1. Soviet Far East (R.S.F.S.R.)—Description and travel. 2. Cub Scouts.]   I. Mason, Charles II. Title.
HS3314.M87   1991
369.43—dc20   90-47498
                                                                                      CIP
                                                                                       AC

Published in the United States by Lodestar Books, an affiliate of Dutton Children's Books, a division of Penguin Books USA Inc.

Published simultaneously in Canada by McClelland & Stewart, Toronto.

Editor: Virginia Buckley   Designer: Kate Nichols

Printed in Hong Kong   First Edition   10 9 8 7 6 5 4 3 2 1

Acknowledgments

We wish to thank the following people:

Svetlana Linnikova, for her friendship and hard work in organizing our visit; the people of Provideniya, especially Nina Nemtseva, Koustautin Roolionov, and the other host families, for opening their arms and homes to the Nome visitors; Mihail Kozakevich, in Provideniya, for coordinating the Cub Scout visit and making it possible; Cubmaster Glenn Martin, for his tireless efforts in successfully bringing about the Cub Scout and Young Pioneer return trips and his help later in clarifying information for this book; Jim Stimpfle, for his dedication and initiative in organizing not only this exchange, but the many others that have since taken place between Nome and Provideniya; U.S. Senator Ted Stevens and his staff, for their efforts in speeding up the involved paperwork process for this trip; Charlie Parr, for his help in the Russian transliterations; Lawrence Kaplan, for his help with Inupiat spellings; Martha Sherwood-Pike, for her assistance with the Cyrillic alphabet; editor Virginia Buckley, for her patient direction; and finally, the eleven Cub Scouts and their parents, for their cooperation and participation in this incredible adventure.

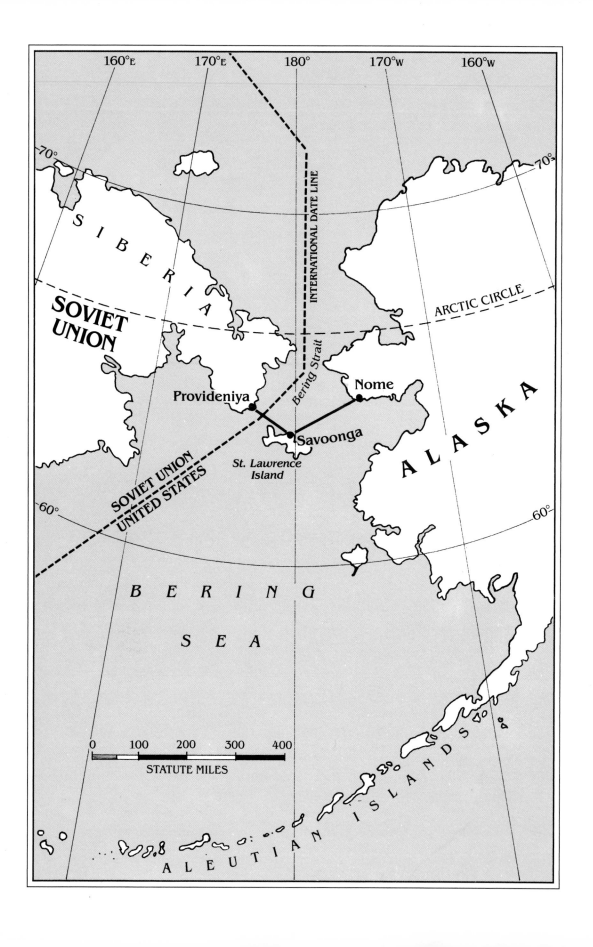

The Cub Scouts in Nome, Alaska, live almost at the top of the world, as far away as you can be from Florida and still be in the United States. They also live on one side of the Bering Strait. On the other side, only two hundred miles across, lies the Soviet Union. It is so close, in fact, that eleven lucky Cub Scouts took a field trip to Provideniya, a small town in the Soviet Far East.

Nome is actually closer to Provideniya than to any other Alaskan town with a Cub Scout pack. The Nome Cub Scouts live in bush Alaska, where there are no roads leading to other towns. The only way to get around is by boat, snow machine, or airplane.

A few years ago Jim Stimpfle, a Nome businessman, began wondering why the people of Nome couldn't be friends with their fellow arctic neighbors. People thought he was crazy because, at that time, Soviets and Americans were forbidden by their governments to travel back and forth without special visas. During World War II, America and the Soviet Union had been allies, but in 1948 because of political problems the two countries closed the border between Alaska and the Soviet Union.

But Jim Stimpfle didn't give up. He kept writing letters to government officials. Finally, both governments gave permission for a friendship visit between the citizens of Provideniya and Nome. The visit was so successful that soon other exchanges were taking place between Alaskans and citizens of the Soviet Far East. Jim Stimpfle and Cubmaster Glenn Martin decided that it was time for a group of young people to go over. So the Cub Scouts and their parents started writing letters to government officials. At last, both governments approved, and the trip

1

was arranged. These scouts would be the first Americans to fly to Provideniya for an extended visit.

Finally, the day of departure arrived. The eleven scouts had packed two small planes with hot dogs and sparklers, to be used in the Fourth of July celebration with the Young Pioneers in Provideniya. They were eager to go, hardly able to stand still patiently in line for their passports and visas. Stephen Busch and his dad, Tom, collected their passports first from Jim Stimpfle, while Ben and Russell Rowe told the rest of the scouts what it was like over there. They had visited Provideniya before with their dad, the owner of Bering Air, which had provided the planes for this flight.

Ben explained, "Hey, it's worth the wait. It's going to be fun. The food is different, but it's good. And everybody is friendly and gives you presents. It's like they're your relatives or something."

CBS News thought that the Cub Scouts's trip to the Soviet Union was so interesting that they had flown out a reporter to cover the story. Many Americans couldn't believe that a group of scouts was being allowed to

visit Provideniya. Ben told the reporter, "Maybe if we go over and become friends, then when we grow up, we can have peace instead of war."

Sean McMillan was embarrassed in front of the microphone and started laughing. Later he said, "I think the reporter wanted us to say we were going to bring the Soviet kids freedom or something. But we just want to get to know them and find out what they're like. I'm kind of nervous, but they're probably scared of meeting us, too."

As the small planes flew over the wide, open tundra and the mountains of Alaska, the scouts settled into their seats. No one talked for awhile. Some were busy with their thoughts, others read the comics.

But soon, from the back of one of the planes, Derek called out, "Hey look. There's St. Lawrence Island, where my mom was born."

Derek and his cousins, Matt and David, are Siberian Yupik Eskimo, with relatives still living on St. Lawrence Island. This remote island is only forty miles from the Soviet Union. For thousands of years, the Siberian Yupik people from both countries often traveled the Bering Strait in *umiaqs* (skin boats) to celebrate potlatches and to trade goods with one another. But that ended in 1948, and the Eskimos didn't understand why.

The boys stared down at the dark blue of the Bering Sea, knowing that once they passed St. Lawrence Island they might spot the Soviet Union. About halfway across the strait, Dave, the pilot, announced, "This is it, boys. We're now officially crossing the international date line. It's no longer the third of July, but rather the *Fourth* of July."

Sean shook his head. "Hey Dave. I know there isn't any line in the sky or anything, but shouldn't I feel something? Isn't there at least going to be a sonic boom?"

Dave turned around, a big smile on his face. "Sorry to disappoint you, boys. The only way you can determine when you are crossing the international date line is by the degrees on the map and by the compass reading. There's nothing to see. But change your watches because we just flew into tomorrow."

And with tomorrow, high, snow-covered mountains and lakes, as wild and empty as Alaska, came into view—the Soviet Union. Suddenly, as the planes flew through glacier valleys, tall buildings and big sailing

ships in port appeared out of nowhere. Provideniya is a seaport town, with over four hundred big ships visiting its docks every year.

Flying into the airport, the scouts stared out the windows in surprise at the writing on the nearby hillsides. Ernie turned back to Therese, the Nome radio announcer who had studied Russian in college. "Therese, what does the writing say?"

" 'Long live Lenin,' and 'Glory to the Soviet Guard.' "

"Does that mean there's going to be fighting?" Ernie's dad shook his head.

When the planes landed at the Ureliki military base, the visitors saw Soviet military planes and helicopters, painted with the red hammer and sickle insignia from the Soviet flag, parked everywhere. The serious guards, dressed in khaki and blue uniforms, stood at attention. The scouts

had been warned that the guards wouldn't smile. Arlo tried his famous grin on the woman who walked him across the runway. He could usually make anyone smile. But not this time.

Arlo felt better when he looked up at the balcony on the airport terminal to find three women smiling and waving, holding a welcome sign in Russian and English.

The boys and their parents were escorted into a cement security waiting area, where the guards checked their luggage and made sure their visas and passports were in order.

A little nervous, the scouts then walked into the main terminal building, to find a huge crowd of people waiting for them, carrying flowers and waving American flags. Soon everyone was smiling and hugging them. The shining sun and the friendliness of the people wiped away the dark, cold feeling of the security area.

For once Sean didn't know what to say. He just stood and stared until Derek whispered, "They don't look any different. The girls are really cute, and the boys look just like Americans." Sean started laughing, his old self again.

The scouts were a little confused because the Young Pioneers weren't wearing their uniforms. Later, they found out that since the pioneers have to wear uniforms all year long in school, in the summertime they enjoy the break and hardly wear them.

Right away, the pioneers converged on the scouts and started giving them little presents like gum and pins, and calling out, "Change. Change." When the scouts and their parents began digging out some of the presents from their backpacks, they were mobbed by even more children. American gum and candy were the most popular items because they are so much sweeter than the Soviet kinds.

Soon the boys had filled their scouting hats and shirts with pins of military stars and photos of Lenin, ski races, and the fiftieth anniversary celebration of Magadon province, where Provideniya is located. The Soviet insignia pins are made of lighter metal and painted more brightly than American ones and are a popular item in Provideniya. The numbers on the Soviet pins were the same as American numbers. The scouts were happy about that because the letters on the pins were written in the Cyrillic alphabet and were difficult to understand (see chart page 40).

Some of the scouts remembered to say *spasibo* (pronounced spa-seeba), thank you, and tried it out when they received a pin. The pioneers smiled and answered back *pozhaluista* (pronounced pazhalsta), you're welcome. On the bus ride into town, the Young Pioneers began to teach the scouts how to pronounce some of the Russian words on the pins. Russian sounds are so different from English sounds that the scouts had a difficult time moving their mouths to make them correctly. Sometimes the words would come out wrong. The pioneers would start laughing, then the scouts joined in.

As soon as they felt brave enough, the pioneers began using some of the English words they had studied in school since the first form (grade).

Stephen told his dad, "I wish I'd studied Russian in school, like they studied English. Then I could talk to them better." His dad was busy looking up words in a Russian/English dictionary, with the help of their hostess, Larisa.

As they rode into Provideniya on the bumpy road, the scouts tried to look around at the scenery, but the pioneers wouldn't let them. After years of practicing English in school, they were eager to try it out on real Americans. When the scouts and Young Pioneers couldn't understand one another, they communicated with sign language and facial expressions.

At the Sports Center, the scouts met their host families and were greeted with welcoming songs. Then Gleb, the son of Svetlana Linnikova, the head of the Young Pioneers, recited a poem in English. "I hope this visit will help the invisible line between our countries disappear," he said. Everyone smiled and clapped loudly.

As they walked down the rocky streets to their host families' homes,

the scouts finally had a chance to look around. It was all so different from Nome. The buildings were old and dark looking, many five stories high and made of cement.

Some of the scouts stopped to play a game of Russian hopscotch, studying the pioneers while they waited their turn. Several were blond, others were dark-haired, and still others had red hair. The girls weren't wearing jeans like the girls in Nome, but they all wore colorful dresses or pants that looked as though they could have been bought in America. The boys wore shirts and sweaters instead of T-shirts, which made them seem a little older than the scouts. But the Soviet children were not much different from the American children after all.

The scouts were staying in flats (apartments) located in the tall buildings scattered around town. The hallways leading to the flats were dark and cold, but inside, the rooms were warm and homey. In almost every home, Oriental rugs hung on the wall and floor for warmth and decoration, and books and delicate china filled the bookshelves. Everything seemed old-fashioned, especially the bathtubs, telephones, and typewriters.

Before they'd even unpacked, David, Stephen, and Derek began playing with Derek's host brother, Denis, and his friend Slava's toy airplanes. The planes were heavier than theirs at home, but just as much fun. Denis is twelve years old and this year was assigned to his first state job. The state provides jobs for all children over twelve during the summer and school vacations. Though there are few cars, Denis is saving his money for a motorcycle like the brightly colored ones occasionally seen on the streets.

After supper, the scouts met at the Tsentur Kultury (Cultural Center) to play games like Duck, Duck, Goose; musical chairs; and Simon Says.

Although the pioneers spoke in Russian and the scouts in English, the actions and rules were exactly the same. The scouts kept laughing because when they covered their ears and didn't hear the Russian words, it was like playing the games back in Nome. Later, den leader Joe Davis took out his Polaroid camera to the delight of some of the Soviet boys, who had never seen a photo develop before their very eyes.

Afterward, when rich cream puffs were served, David whispered to his mother, "These are even better than *akutaq* (Eskimo ice cream) or chocolate ice cream." Angela smiled. Her son should know. He really liked to eat.

After the games, the adults began visiting with one another. Some of the scouts took out their plastic toy transformers, rapidly changing the army figures into track vehicles or airplanes while the pioneers watched mesmerized. The scouts were surprised to learn that the Soviet boys had never seen any before. Matt Metcalf said to pioneers Gleb and Dmitry, "Here, take mine. You've got to have a transformer. Everybody in Nome has one."

16

On the way out of the Cultural Center, the scouts stopped to look at the display of children's artwork. They were amazed to find pictures of whales, boats, flowers, and children playing—just the sort of pictures children draw in Nome.

The light streaming through the windows that night didn't bother the scouts. Since Provideniya is on the same degree of latitude as Nome, the midnight sun shines brightly in both towns this time of year, providing almost continuous daylight in the summertime.

On their boat ride up Emma Bay the next morning, the children played on deck, the wind blowing in their faces. When they got cold, Jake and Sean moved inside the cabin and began singing silly American songs to Olla and Katia, who in turn kept putting up two fingers like bunny ears behind their heads. The boys had met their match.

After the boat ride, everyone walked over to the Provideniya museum. On the way, some of the scouts and pioneers started throwing around a Frisbee. Although they'd never seen a Frisbee before, the pioneers caught on quickly. One time it landed right in front of Lenin's statue.

In the museum, items from the early history of Provideniya and Soviet Eskimo arts and crafts were displayed. The beaded sealskin slippers
and *kuspuk* jackets were similar to the ones that the relatives of the
Eskimo scouts make and wear. Arlo signed the museum guestbook. He
was wearing the white *kuspuk* his Inupiaq Eskimo grandmother had
made especially for this trip.

The museum also had a special room filled with objects such as pins,
photographs, and even a Nome T-shirt from previous friendship exchanges between Nome and Provideniya. "I hope something from our

trip is displayed after we leave," Derek said. "How about the Frisbee?" On the way out, he handed the Frisbee to the museum director.

Obed, the midday meal, was served at the *kantina* (cafeteria). There are only two restaurants in Provideniya, and they are used mostly by state workers at lunchtime. The scouts were surprised to learn that many Soviet people would rather eat at home. Actually, *obed* is more like an American dinner because the Soviets eat their biggest meal of the day at noon. The scouts filled up on borscht—a Russian soup made of beets, milk, and chunks of beef—cucumber salad, and beef Stroganoff with rice. Jake liked the Stroganoff so much that he had seconds. The boys also became fond of the bottled lemonade Soviet children drink instead of soda pop.

There were relay races in the Sports Hall after lunch. The slogan on the wall inspired all the young athletes to do their best. Russell Rowe said to his mom, "Our Cub Scout slogan says the same thing—'to do our best.' "

The mixed teams of Cub Scouts and Young Pioneers competed enthusiastically, while the adults and younger children yelled on the sidelines. Later, all the children challenged the adults to a tug of war, the children winning by a landslide.

After the games, the scouts finally had some free time to walk around town and shop. Wherever they went, the children of Provideniya came out to join them.

The scouts had rubles to spend because the Soviet bank had given them one ruble for every $1.60 in American money they exchanged. Trying to keep track of the cost of things confused the boys at first, but with so many unusual items to buy, it was worth the trouble.

Arlo headed for the toy store. He looked over the blocks, books, puzzles, and cars and trucks with his new friend Tolya. Arlo was surprised to find no electronic or computerized toys. Like all the stores in Provideniya, the toy store was small and dimly lit. Without computers and loudspeakers, it was really quiet.

Tolya helped Arlo pick out some books and an airplane. While the saleswoman wrapped Arlo's purchases in brown paper and tied them with string, he said to his dad, "I wonder why American toys have so much extra packaging."

Tolya then took Arlo and his dad to the music store, where Arlo's dad wanted to look at all the handmade instruments. He bought a small violin for Arlo and a concertina for himself. A concertina is like a small accordion.

Meanwhile, Derek went to the fabric store with his dad. When Derek brought his purchases up to the counter, the saleswoman wrote down the prices on a piece of paper and then added them up on an abacus. Derek had never seen an abacus before and didn't even know how it worked. He stared in amazement as the woman moved the beads quickly to come up with the total. On the way out, his dad told Derek, "I

remember using an abacus in school when I was your age, but I haven't seen one in a long time." Derek kept shaking his head. How could she figure up the total with just a set of beads?

Later, Derek's mom joined him and his dad. They looked in at the food store, but didn't shop because there were hardly any goods on the shelves. Afterward, Derek asked Svetlana, the head of the pioneers, why the shelves were so empty. "There are many people and not enough factories and farms to produce all the goods and food they need and want. The government regulates how much food is sent into Provideniya. The officials are working on providing more goods for the people to buy, but for now we have to be satisfied that we have enough to eat."

On the street as they went back to their homes, the scouts passed some kiosks. Teenage girls open up the booths every afternoon and sell items such as combs, toothpaste, and toys. Some kiosks sell only newspapers or flowers. They look like American hot dog stands, but these kiosks never sell food because, remember, the Soviets don't eat out much.

In many places around Provideniya, cement steps are built into the hillsides, making it easier to walk down into the center of town. There are few cars in Provideniya because they are so expensive and the dirt roads aren't very good. People walk everywhere, and the steps provide a good rest spot. Seth sat on one while he waited for his parents to finish buying presents.

Derek and the other scouts were hungry after all the shopping, so at their host family's home, his dad brought out the American popcorn he had been saving for just the right moment. He let some of the pioneers heat it up on the gas stove. They watched with delight as it expanded into a huge silver bubble. During the popcorn party, the adults kept trying to communicate, flipping frantically through their Russian and American dictionaries. But the children still preferred their own way of communicating—laughing, pointing, and sign language.

At one point, Cubmaster Glenn Martin interrupted to explain, "Right now, we are all experiencing *druzhba* (pronounced droozba), the true

25

meaning of friendship." The boys started laughing, and the adults smiled and nodded their heads.

The dancing and singing that evening was especially important to David, Matt, and Derek, and their mothers. Several of their Siberian Yupik relatives had traveled from Old Chaplino, a nearby Eskimo village, to meet them. The boys' mothers began speaking quickly in Siberian Yupik. Their relatives understood them, several breaking into broad smiles, others crying. It had been over forty years since the Siberian Yupiks had been able to meet their Alaskan relatives.

The Soviet Eskimos reached out and hugged their American nephews. One older woman said to Derek in Siberian Yupik, "Young man, I remember playing with your grandfather in Savoonga on St. Lawrence Island many years ago. But then they closed the border, and I've never seen him since."

Derek can't speak Siberian Yupik, but he understood some of the words. His mother translated the rest for him and explained that this woman was his grandfather's sister-in-law.

Later, the three mothers got up and danced with their relatives. This dance had been performed by their ancestors at potlatches for hundreds of years before the border was closed.

The celebration went on late into the night. The Alaskans sang "God Bless America," and the Provideniyans joined in. Then some visitors from Moscow sang "Moscow Nights," and everyone sang that also. Everyone felt like family. People kept handing the scouts presents, telling them how happy they were to have them visit.

The scouts were greeted just as warmly the next morning when they visited a summer camp at a school in Ureliki. As they walked into the school, all the children lined the hallway, clapping and cheering. The school had even been freshly painted for this honored visit. The girls were dressed up in their very best ruffled dresses and fancy bows.

The Ureliki children handed the scouts books, toys, and other presents. The scouts said *spasibo* and kept smiling, but by now they were embarrassed by all the generosity and had long since run out of their own gifts to give.

Everyone was ushered into a nearby classroom for a performance. The scouts kept looking around at the familiar school setting with its chalkboards, desks, and student work on display. But the Cyrillic alpha-

bet around the room and the Soviet flag reminded them that this wasn't Nome after all.

The campers began singing Russian and American songs. Then the youngest camper, Nadia, a beautiful six-year-old wearing a bow as big as her head, recited a poem in perfect English.

> "Good morning to you,
> Good morning to you,
> I'm so glad to see you,
> Good morning to you."

The scouts's enthusiastic applause reflected their admiration for this little girl, who had mastered English so well.

In the cafeteria, they were served cookies along with tea brewed in the gleaming, silver samovars saved for special occasions. Then, suddenly, the Soviet children burst into one of their favorite songs, written by a little Moscow boy many years ago. Some of the scouts also knew it because the American folksinger Pete Seeger had made the song popular in America when he recorded it on one of his albums. The room filled with voices singing in unison in both Russian and English.

"May there always be sunshine,
May there always be blue skies,
May there always be mama,
May there always be me."

On the second verse, the scouts tried singing it in Russian, and the pioneers and campers tried in English, following along with the song leaders.

Because it was raining outside, the festivities moved on to the gym for games. Some children started climbing a hanging rope, just like the one in Nome's school gym, while others climbed the wall ladders.

Cubmaster Glenn Martin climbed up a rope and left his scout hat at the top. A pioneer climbed up right behind him and grabbed it, and everyone started cheering. When the boy came back down, Glenn said he could keep the hat. At this, scouts and pioneers began trading their gear. On the other side of the gym, some children began playing Simple Simon.

To top off the morning, the scout den leaders organized a game of softball, the only American game the Soviet children had never played. Although the Soviet boys hadn't swung a bat before, they caught on quickly. The spectators, including the Soviet girls—who didn't want to play—cheered wildly whenever the ball was hit. The scouts asked for the Russian word for softball, but none exists. Ben Rowe smiled. "Maybe they'll make one up, now that they know how to play."

All the campers walked the visitors to the door to say good-bye. One of the teachers told the scouts, "You are the first American children we've ever seen. Thank you so much for coming."

In spite of the rain, excitement grew on the bus ride home in anticipation of the long-awaited hot dog cookout. As they hiked up the steep hillside behind Provideniya, the scouts and pioneers carried wood for the fire. At the very top of the hill overlooking Emma Bay, they built a huge bonfire and warmed their hands. Then out came the hot dogs to

be roasted on long wooden sticks the pioneers had carved for the occasion. The pioneers often roast shish kebabs of meat and vegetables outside over the fire in wintertime. They all crowded around the fire to try their first American hot dog. They especially liked the soft hot dog buns and mild mustard and ketchup.

To complete the feast, the scouts and pioneers toasted marshmallows. The pioneers had never tasted such sweet stuff over a fire before. Then the scouts distributed Fourth of July sparklers to their new friends. The young people excitedly lit them and then ran up and down the hillside, twirling them in the air.

Even though it was rainy and cold, no one wanted to leave. One of the pioneers lent David a bike, which he rode all over the hillside, with a large group of children chasing him from behind. Finally, David gave up the bike to Sean. He explained, "It's not as fancy as mine, but it's just as much fun." As he watched Sean ride away, he said to the other scouts, "I felt pretty shy at first, but now they're my friends."

On the final evening, the pioneers practiced their English one more time and asked last-minute questions about Alaska and America. Derek said to Sergei, "You'll have to come visit us. My dad's already invited all of you. We could show you our school and our computers, and the gold mine and all our stores."

Sergei smiled. Then he said seriously, "I want to very much, but over here we have to obtain special passes before we can travel. Sometimes it takes months for them to come through."

"Oh, you'll come," said Derek. "When my dad really wants something, he makes sure it happens. He's already set it up for September, and Svetlana is working on it, so I *know* you'll come."

At the final get-together, the pioneers showed movies of themselves swimming and hiking at their summer camp and of the winter carnival ski races. Later, some Young Pioneers performed Ukrainian folk dances. This was followed by a modern dance recital given by the girls.

Seth whispered to his mother, "Some of the girls in Nome dance like that."

"We're so much more alike than we ever imagined, aren't we?"

The next morning, the people of Provideniya hugged the scouts good-bye, while the pioneers handed out flowers and last-minute presents. Because of the bad weather, the flight was delayed for awhile, so to pass the time, the scouts and pioneers gathered around the television and watched cartoons. Laughing, Jake exclaimed, "These are really funny. My dad says they are like American cartoons from the 1950s."

Arlo agreed. "And my dad wishes we still had cartoons like these because they aren't so violent."

Finally, the weather cleared. As David and Derek stood at the door of the small plane, the Young Pioneers hung on the barbed wire fence, waving good-bye and calling out, *"Das vidaniya, das vidaniya."* Not good-bye, but "until we meet again."

On the flight home, Stephen turned to his dad and asked, "Will we meet them again? I want to see Larisa and everybody again. They're our friends now."

"I'd say they're more like family, son. Yes, we'll meet them again."

When the scouts returned home, they realized that, in four short days, they had forgotten the noise of the cars driving down Front Street. They'd also forgotten how busy the stores were and how many more items they carried. Not thinking, one scout tried to buy a soda pop with a leftover ruble.

Many Nomites wanted to know what it was like over in Provideniya. The Cub Scouts told them that it was terrific and that they should go and see for themselves. A group of Girl Scouts did go over in August, and when they returned, they worked as hard as the Cub Scouts to make sure that the return visit of the Young Pioneers really happened.

Despite all the letters and plans, some people still said the Soviet government would never allow young people to visit Nome. But they were proven wrong when in September, just as Derek had predicted, the Young Pioneers arrived, with much hugging and crying like any family reunion. While the adults caught up on news, the scouts and Young Pioneers hurried off to swim, play computer games, visit the video arcade, take a dogsled ride, tour one of the biggest gold dredges in the world, and, of course, shop. The pioneers couldn't believe all there was to buy.

Each pioneer had his or her favorite activity. Anna explained, "For me it was the computers because we don't have any in Provideniya. Imagine, a room full of computers!"

What the scouts enjoyed most was seeing their new friends again and introducing them to their old friends in Nome. As in Provideniya, the whole town of Nome welcomed the Young Pioneers with celebrations, including an evening at the ice cream parlor and an evening of singing and dancing.

As she was leaving, Larisa summed up the feelings of all the pioneers and their parents. "I couldn't believe how friendly everyone was. Of course, the stores are great, but the people are even better."

The number of visits between residents of Nome and Provideniya and other citizens of Alaska and the Soviet Far East is growing every day. A recent treaty between the United States and the Soviet Union now allows Eskimos in both Alaska and the Soviet Far East to visit relatives across the Bering Strait without special permission.

Eleven lucky Cub Scouts were able to discover, while still young, that people are people no matter where you go. Like the Berlin Wall, the barriers between the Soviet Union and the United States are coming down, and a true bridge of friendship has been built. These children from neighboring arctic regions across the international date line have helped make that happen. They have come to know and care about one another in a very real way and to learn that peace may indeed be a possibility in our lifetime.

Cyrillic Alphabet

Letters	Names of Letters	Equivalent sounds in English
А, а	ah	*f*ather
Б, б	beh	*b*et
В, в	veh	*v*at
Г, г	ggeh	*g*o
Д, д	deh	*d*am
Е, е	yeh	*ye*t
Ё, ё	yoh	*yaw*n
Ж, ж	zheh	plea*s*ure
З, з	zeh	*z*one
И, и	ee	*ee*l
Й, й	ee KRAHT-koh-yeh	bo*y*
К, к	kah	*k*ick
Л, л	el	*l*ow
М, м	em	*m*et
Н, н	en	*n*et
О, о	oh	t*oy*, sp*or*t
П, п	peh	*p*et
Р, р	er	d*r*ead (trilled *r*)
С, с	es	*s*ell
Т, т	teh	*t*ell
У, у	oo	m*oo*n
Ф, ф	ef	*f*un
Х, х	khah	lo*ch*, soft sound *H*ugo
Ц, ц	tseh	ca*ts*
Ч, ч	chah	*ch*urch
Ш, ш	shah	*sh*ip
Щ, щ	shchah	prolonged *sh* sound
ъ	tv'YOR-dee znahk	indicates hard stress on previous consonant
ы	yeh-REE	s*i*t
ь	m'YAH-kee znahk	no sound, indicates soft emphasis
Э, э	eh (oh-boh-ROHT-noh-yeh)	p*e*t
Ю, ю	yoo	*yu*le
Я, я	yah	*ya*rd

Glossary

Akutaq Eskimo dessert, commonly known as Eskimo ice cream, made with whitefish, seal oil, and berries

Flat Apartment or suite of rooms

Inupiat Eskimo people from northern Alaska and Canada who speak the Inupiaq language

Kuspuk Eskimo word for garment that can be designed and worn as a jacket, dress, or blouse

Lenin Leader of the 1917 Soviet revolution in which the Russian people overthrew the czar and formed the Communist government. He is known as the father of the USSR.

Magadon Province or state in the Soviet Far East. Provideniya is a small town in the province of Magadon.

Samovar A Russian metal pot with internal tube for heating water for tea, usually made out of silver

Siberian Yupik Eskimo people from Siberia in the Soviet Union and northwestern Alaska, who speak the same Siberian Yupik language

Tundra Any of the vast, treeless arctic plains (originally a Russian word)

Visa Endorsement on a passport, giving permission to enter a country